THE SECRET OF 13

by B.B. HILLER

illustrated by BERT DODSON

D0937657

SCHOLASTIC INC.

New York Toronto London Auckland Sydney

ISBN 0-590-33294-5

12 11 10 9 8 7 6 5 4 3 2   2 3 4 5/9

Printed in the U.S.A.   40

For Neil
—of course

Scholastic Books in the Pick-A-Path Series
How many have you read?

READ THIS FIRST

Are you ready for some really fantastic adventures?

Start reading on **page 1** and keep going until you have to make a choice. Then decide what you want to do and turn to that page.

Keep going until you reach **THE END.** Then, you can go back and start again. Every path leads to a new story!

It is all up to you!

You've just gotten some terrific news: The dentist says, "No cavities." No matter how hard he tried, he couldn't find anything in your mouth to drill. You're free! You feel like you're walking on air, even though you're just 15 floors up in the Medical Arts Building.

You check your great-grandfather's pocket watch because you're meeting your mother and your little brother in the lobby. Then you're off with them to have lunch and, if there's time, to see *It Came From Beyond Mars*. That's what your mom promised if you didn't have any cavities. She'll be surprised to learn she's really going to have to go!

You walk onto the elevator and push *L* for lobby, but the elevator slows and stops at 13.

Turn to **page 2.**

2 When the doors open on 13, you are blinded by bright lights and can hardly see anything. The form of a man appears at the elevator door. His left hand reaches to you. You see he's holding some paper. The elevator door begins to close. The man seems to say "Please!" and shoves the paper at you. You grab it just in time!

Go on to the next page.

When the door is shut, you realize **3**
that instead of just taking the paper
from the man, you should have *also*
pushed another button on the elevator
— but which one?

DOOR OPEN?
Turn to
page 4.

DOOR CLOSE?
Turn to
page 10.

TWELFTH
FLOOR?
Turn to
page 6.

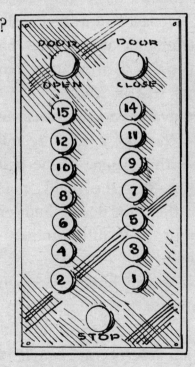

4   Maybe you can *still* open the door. Quickly, you reach for DOOR OPEN, but it's too late. The doors close and the elevator heads down.

You look at the envelope that creepy guy handed you. On one side, in big black letters, it says: DO NOT OPEN.

Swell, a chance in a lifetime for some real excitement and you're not supposed to open it. You turn it over. It says: THIS MEANS YOU!

The elevator door opens and you step into the lobby. "You're not going to believe this, Mom. In the first place, no cavities. But the really weird stuff starts on the 13th floor!" Suddenly you realize your sweet little brother, Henry, has grabbed the envelope!

Can you stop him from opening it? Do you *want* to?

If you let Henry open it, turn to **page 17.**
If you stop him from opening it, turn to **page 20.**

6   Quickly, you push 12. When the elevator door opens, you get off so you can walk back up to 13. You want to see what's really happening. You stick the mysterious paper into your pocket for safekeeping. The stairs are right by the elevator, so within seconds, you are back up on . . .

Wait a minute!

You were on 12. You only walked up one flight of stairs. But this sure isn't the same place you saw from the elevator! In fact, it looks like something from a museum! It's an antique office. There are rows and rows of battered oak desks. The people sitting at them are wearing old-fashioned clothes and green eyeshades. They are dipping pens in inkwells in their desk-tops!

Go on to the next page.

Boy, did *you* ever get a wrong number. It must have been *14* where the lights were and the guy handed you the paper. You'd better get up there fast. That man was in trouble and needs your help!

How do you want to go upstairs?

Elevator? Turn to **page 11.**
Stairs? Turn to **page 8.**

8   There's the door to the stairwell. You race up the stairs to the 14th floor. Out of breath, you push open the stair door to find . . . nothing.

At least, it's nothing like the place you saw from the elevator. In fact, it looks just like your dentist's floor. In fact, it *is* your dentist's floor — and there's your little brother Henry.

"Henry, what are you doing here?"

"Mom sent me up to find you. She couldn't leave the car to come up herself because she's double-parked." Now you know why Henry's there. What you don't know is how you got to 15 by coming up one flight from 13. Oh, well, maybe your mind was wandering. Maybe that's why you were so out of breath when you got to 15. Maybe you're just imagining the whole thing. You decide to get on the elevator and leave this place.

Go on to the next page.

Well, perhaps it couldn't hurt just to *stop* at 14 and 13 on your way down. You decide to do that and tell Henry to push the buttons. He *loves* to push elevator buttons.

"But I can't do it," he says.

"Of course you can," you say. What a baby Henry can be sometimes.

"No, I can't. There *is* no 13."

"*Sure* there is." You go to show him. "Look, just push — " Henry's right. There's *no* 13! What *is* going on here?

If you think you just got confused when you left the dentist's office and you should forget all of this and go to the movie with your mother,
turn to **page 14.**
If you think there's a logical explanation for this,
turn to **page 13.**

DOOR CLOSE? Where's your sense of adventure? If you don't like bright lights, creepy guys, strange papers, and 13th floors, this might as well be

THE END

P.S. Or you could go back to page 3 and pick another button to push.

Okay, so you're going to take the elevator to 14, but it seems there's a little problem with this — there's no elevator! You know *exactly* where it should be. It's in the same place on every floor. How could it *not* be on this floor? Right where there *ought* to be an elevator, there's a large supply cabinet! Oh, well, you can still take the stairs. You know where those are because you came up on them from 12. As you turn to take the stairs, you see a boy about your age, wearing sort of old-fashioned clothes.

"Hi," you say.

"Good afternoon," he answers. "Is there something I can help you with?"

"Well, I was looking for the elevator — "

"The what?"

"The elevator — you know — to go out."

Turn to **page 12.**

12   "If you want to go out, why don't you use that? It's called a door."

Then the boy points to a door — to the outside! You are on the ground floor!

The boy stares at you with the same "Is-this-some-kind-of-a-nut?" look that you'd been planning to give *him*.

"Come, now," the boy says, just a bit too patiently. "I'll show you how it works. You just take hold of the knob, turn, and push out."

"That's not the problem. It's just that a minute ago. . ."

Now, think a bit. Is this kid going to believe you if you tell him he's on the 13th floor and that door ought to be an elevator? Do you really think so?

Okay, go ahead and try it,
on **page 42.**
On the other hand, if you think he
might be able to tell you *something,*
turn to **page 56.**

Looking for page 13? In most elevators, and in this book, there is no 13!

"Okay, Henry," you say. "Let's just go down to Mom." Henry pushes *L* and you're on your way.

Then you remember the paper the man handed you. No matter *what* floor it was, that *did* happen, right? Now, where is the paper? Oh, yeah, you put it in your pocket. You pull it out and see that it's the front page of a newspaper. *Hmmmmmmm. That's strange,* you think, looking at the headlines:

Turn to **page 15.**

15   How could something like that have happened without your knowing about it? It must have happened a long time ago — now, wait a minute! This article is about the Medical Arts Building. You're *in* the Medical Arts Building and it's *not* rubble. You look again. The date on the newspaper is — it couldn't be, but it *is*. It's tomorrow's paper!

Quickly, you read more of the story. It's so interesting you barely notice the man next to you who is holding something cupped in his hand.

According to the news story, the Fire Chief suspects the fire began with a cigarette tossed carelessly in the elevator. Later, something else caught fire from the cigarette. No one was hurt, but the building was destroyed. Completely.

Go on to the next page.

The elevator stops at the lobby. You **16**
fold the newspaper and stick it in your
pocket before the door opens. You and
Henry step off the elevator first. Before the door closes behind the man,
you see him drop something in the
elevator.

*If you think the man could use a
reminder about littering,*

turn to **page 58.**

If you believe tomorrow's paper,

turn to **page 50.**

17   *Rrrrrrip!* Henry shakes the opened envelope and out comes . . .

"Henry!" you say. "What *is* it?"

It's a piece of paper — an *old* piece of paper. You go to look at it more closely, before Henry tears it to pieces. It's a map, and it looks like this:

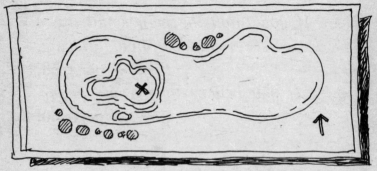

"What's that?" asks your mother.

"I know! I know!" said Henry. "It's the blueberry place!"

The blueberry place? Oh, yeah, he *could* mean that little island where you went to pick blueberries last year. That was in the pond in Harrison Park, somewhere near the edge of town. Could Henry be right about the map? He's pretty smart for a little kid, you think.

Go on to the next page.

You look more closely. Henry *could* be right. But what does the X mean?

Could it be . . . something buried? Do you believe that's not really Blueberry Island, but *Treasure* Island?

You bet you do!

"Come on, Mom, Henry! Let's go dig up the treasure!"

"Excuse me," says the doorman. "I couldn't help overhearing you. I think you've made a mountain out of a molehill. Why, I've been on Blueberry Island, and I'm sure that X marks the location of the biggest blueberry bush on the island. There's no treasure there. What do you think this is? A pirate story?"

Now *there's* an idea.

If you think this is a pirate story, turn to **page 29.**
If you're pretty sure it's another kind of adventure, turn to **page 35.**

"Henry! You shouldn't open that. It could be dangerous!"

Henry dutifully hands you the envelope. You stick it in your jacket pocket for later. Now, however, *It Came From Beyond Mars* is about to start.

"Let's forget this envelope for now and get to the movie!" Your mother seems strangely enthusiastic.

"Great idea! Let's go!" You get into the car. On the way to the theater, you think out loud, "Some day I'd like to have a computer with — "

"Why *some* day?" asks your mother. She makes a screeching U-turn into an electronics store. "What's the matter with *now*?"

" — with a disk drive, a four-color plotter/printer, and a 256K memory — what did you say?" You think there's something wrong with your hearing.

"I said why wait? You want those things, so we'll get them. Now."

Turn to **page 21.**

21   "Well," you say uncertainly. "I thought we'd go to the movie now."

"Whatever you say, darling." She turns again. That's strange, but sometimes grown-ups *are* strange.

At the movie theater, you and Henry go to the refreshment stand.

"I can't decide between popcorn, soda, chocolate nut caramels, red licorice, or peanut butter cups. Or chocolate raisins," you tell your mother.

"One of each," she tells the man.

"Can I have some fruit chews?" asks Henry.

"No," your mother answers simply.

In the quiet before the movie starts, you decide there's something magical about the envelope, but how could it have power over your mother? Maybe it's just your imagination.

If you think it's magic,
turn to **page 23.**
If you think you've lost your
marbles, turn to **page 27.**

This is a pretty country road. It must be near Harrison Park, right?

Up ahead, you see a sign. Can you make out the letters? Not quite. Oh, yes, now it's clear. You blew it and this is

THE

Sure it's magic. What else would make your mother behave that way? You're so excited by the prospects that you can hardly sit still through the movie.

On your way home, you test your theory.

"You know, Mom, I've always thought it would be fun to go to Hawaii — "

"The travel agency is closed now, but we can call in the morning. Would vacation time be soon enough or do you want to take time off from school?" *Hmmmmm.*

Go on to the next page.

"Vacation will be soon enough," you say. No point in pushing this. "Besides, I'd like some new clothes first."

"We'll stop at the mall now. It's just on the other side of the river. What do you want?"

"Well, I — " You look at your jacket on the seat next to you. "I could use a new jacket."

"Yes," says your mother. "I've always disliked that one." She reaches over the seat and grabs the jacket. Suddenly, she rolls down her window and flings the jacket out. As you watch it fall into the waters of the river, you remember the envelope! It's in the pocket!

Turn to **page 25.**

25   "Mom! My jacket!"

"What's the matter with you?" she asks, annoyed. "Why did you throw it out the window?"

"Me?! You were going to buy me a new one before my trip to Hawaii! Hey, there's another electronics store. We can get the computer now!"

"New jacket? Hawaii? Computer? What are you talking about? Do you think we're made of money? It's a good thing you can still fit into last year's jacket because you're going to have to wear it now. That is, if you *can* still fit into it, considering all the candy you ate at the movie! And right after seeing the dentist, too! There's something else I've been meaning to tell you . . . ." and on she goes. Just like normal. Your worst fears are realized.

Go on to the next page.

So the envelope really *was* magic.
It was nice while it lasted.

A thought crosses your mind. You will have another dentist appointment in six months. Maybe, just maybe, the elevator will stop on 13 again!

THE END

27 *That's right*, you think. *There's no such thing as magic.* Your mother really didn't say you could get a 256K computer, disk drive, and four-color plotter/printer. She probably didn't even buy you all that candy. She never made a U-turn on a major street in her life.

There, now don't you feel better? There *is* a reason for all that weird stuff. You made it up!

Go on to the next page.

After the movie is over, you get into the car to drive back home. On your way, you remember the envelope. You pull it out of your pocket and look at it. What kind of nonsense is that DO NOT OPEN/THIS MEANS YOU stuff? There can't be anything all that important in it — certainly nothing magical! You tear open the envelope and find a small piece of paper in it. It reads:

YOU ARE VERY LUCKY THAT YOU EXPECT NOTHING.

YOU WILL NEVER BE DISAPPOINTED.

See? You were right. There was no magic. Or was there? Well, too late now. It's

THE END

Sure, it *must* be a pirate story. Where else do you find treasure maps with X's on them? But just where is Harrison Park? You turn the paper over. The other side reads:

TO GET TO HARRISON PARK:

Follow Main Street and bear right at traffic light.
Turn left at church.
Turn right at the Post Office.
Pass school on your left.
Harrison Park is third right.

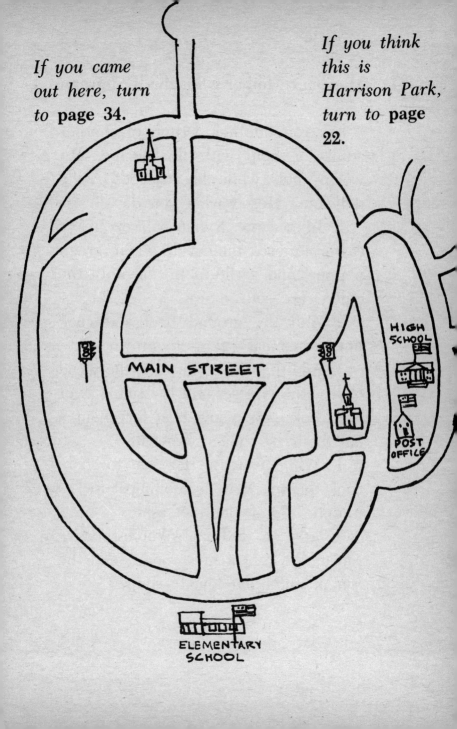

If you came out here, turn to **page 34**.

If you think this is Harrison Park, turn to **page 22**.

MAIN STREET

HIGH SCHOOL

POST OFFICE

ELEMENTARY SCHOOL

Ask your mother, father, or another adult for help with this recipe. It's worth their while because it's *really* delicious. Here's what you do:

1. In a large frying pan or heavy casserole, cook the cut-up onion, green pepper, and garlic in the oil until the onions are soft.

2. Add the ground beef and cook until the meat begins to brown.

3. Add the can of tomatoes, the sliced olives, the cheese, and the salt. Cover and cook over a low heat for about a half hour, stirring occasionally.

4. While you wait for that to cook, cook the spaghetti by boiling it for 10 minutes. Drain and set aside.

5. Add a dash of Worcestershire sauce, the can of mushrooms, and the can of *undiluted* tomato soup.

Go on to the next page.

6. Mix all ingredients well, then combine with the cooked spaghetti in a large, covered casserole.

7. Let the casserole cool and then put it in the refrigerator for at least a day. Before you serve it, bake in a covered dish for an hour at 350 degrees.

Of course, you *can* eat it right away, but it really tastes much better if you keep it a day in the refrigerator. This will feed 6 hungry people.

What's the secret of 13, you ask? It's the great dinner you get from these 13 ingredients!

THE END

You did a nice job of navigating through that map and those instructions! There's Harrison Park, and there, to the right, is the pond. You go to the edge and, luckily, there is a rowboat there. You, Henry, and your mother climb in and row to the island.

Very carefully, you orient yourselves to the treasure map. Exactly where the X says it will be, there's a freshly dug mound of earth! Could it really be a treasure trove? You each grab something to dig with and very quickly you find an old chest. You pull it out of the hole and open it to discover a true pirate treasure! Silver, gold, emeralds, rubies, diamonds, pearls — riches beyond your wildest imaginings!

Who ever said 13 was unlucky? To you, it's

THE END

35   "Now, now, kids," says your mother, somewhat annoyed. "That's not a treasure map. There's no such *thing* as a treasure map. That paper is just scribbling."

You look more closely and you have to agree with your mother. Even if it *is* a treasure map, which it certainly *isn't*, it's not *really* the pond in Harrison Park. Disappointed, you turn the "map" over. It reads:

1 onion	½ cup grated
1 green pepper	Parmesan
1 clove garlic	cheese
5 tbs. vegetable	1½ tsp. salt
oil	Worcestershire
1 lb. ground	sauce
beef	1 can mush-
1 lg. can toma-	rooms
toes	1 can tomato
½ cup sliced	soup
stuffed olives	½ lb. spaghetti

Go on to the next page.

Worcestershire sauce! Wait a second, there. This was supposed to be an adventure story, not a cooking class!

If you still think this is an adventure story and if you want to try your luck with the pirates and look for the treasure,
turn to **page 29.**
If you think this list of ingredients could be some kind of code,
turn to **page 37.**
If you'd like to try this recipe,
turn to **page 31.**

37 "Look at this, Mom," you say.

"*Hmmm,*" she says. "Now, that sounds delicious! Just what we'll have for dinner. Here's some money so you and Henry can go to the supermarket while I'm in the beauty parlor."

As you walk to the supermarket, you try to figure out a way around eating mushrooms for dinner.

With Henry's help and suggestions, the shopping trip is a breeze. You pay for the groceries and are about to leave.

Suddenly, two guys steal your groceries and run like crazy. You and Henry take off after them, but they disappear. Then two *other* men run up to you and Henry.

One of them says, "Why didn't you stop them? The security of your country is in danger!"

Now, *that's* adventure!

Turn to **page 39.**

39 "Huh? Security?! They stole our dinner!"

"What do you mean they stole your dinner?" the man asks.

Patiently, you explain. "Mom was going to make dinner with the recipe from the envelope I got on the 13th floor of the Medical Arts Building."

"That was no dinner! We are government agents and that list is a top secret coded message. It gives the password to Fort Knox and the combination of the safe that holds all of the United States' gold! Anyone who can crack the code can steal all of our gold bullion!"

"Well, here's the list," you say, pulling it out of your pocket. You hand it to them.

"But *they* have the groceries — they know what was on the list! And they are spies from a country that would just *love* to steal our gold!"

Go on to the next page.

"Do you think they'll mind about the mushrooms?" asks Henry.

"I don't know," you tell him. "And remember, not *everybody* likes maple syrup on spaghetti. Those guys could be really mad at us."

"They'll probably like the sausage, though."

"Maybe, but you know, Henry," you say, "I'm just as glad that stuff got stolen. I don't think Mom would have been too crazy about the jalapeño peppers we got instead of the olives."

"Hey, kids," says one of the agents. "Are you telling us that you *didn't* buy the items on this list?"

"Of course not. A lot of that stuff is really gross," you explain.

"Then we're saved! The gold in Fort Knox will *stay* in Fort Knox. You kids are heroes! How can we reward you?"

You and Henry think a bit.

Turn to **page 41.**

41   "I know," you tell them. "Come up with something else for dinner. Something *without* mushrooms in it."

"It's a deal."

That night, the men take you and your family out to dinner. You have spaghetti with sausage and jalapeño pepper sauce and, for Henry, the chef prepares spaghetti and maple syrup. That hero's meal is

THE END

"Here's what happened," you begin. **42**
"I was in the elevator, coming down
from 15. Mom and Henry, my brother,
were waiting downstairs, double-parked.
We were going to see *It Came From
Beyond Mars* at the movies. Have you
seen it?"

The boy looks at you strangely, then
says, "I do not understand what you
are saying. What do you mean — *coming down from 15, car, double-parked,
movies*? Who are you?"

You realize this place may call for
closer examination. On your second
look, you begin to piece it together
— and you don't like it at all!

"What's the date?" you ask.

"July 1, 1912."

Oh, no! Somehow, that 13th floor
got you to travel back in time! But
how can you get back now? Why don't
you try the staircase again?

Turn to **page 43.**

43   "I, uh, think I'd better go now," you say and move quickly to the door that leads to the stairs. Soon you are through it and you breathe a sigh of relief. Then you remember that you really ought to have said good-bye, or thank you, or something.

You pull the door open again, but the boy is gone. So are the oak desks and the pens and inkwells. Now the room is filled with people dressed the way they did in the 1950s. Some of the women are wearing skirts with poodles on them, and the men have crew cuts! You are so astonished that the door slips shut again.

Unable to believe what you saw, you open the door again, this time to — the outdoors! There are trees and rocks and birds and a creek and — this must be what it was like before the town was built! Every time you open the door, it's a different time!

Go on to the next page.

You open the door and close it again and again, but each time the scene is different and nothing looks familiar! How many times will you have to open the door before you get to your *own* time? This is as good a time as any to find out, because until you do, it's

THE END

45   So, you're going to try your luck in 1912. You figure that since you got here, you can surely get back, right?

This boy seems nice. You introduce yourself to him. He puts out his hand to shake and says, "Call me Buddy. Everyone does — except my mother." For some reason, he seems almost familiar to you, but of *course* you've never met. How could you have?

Go on to the next page.

You and Buddy hit it off at once. **46**
You talk a bit and he shows you his
marble collection. You show him your
great-grandfather's watch which you
have with you. He takes you on a tour
of the town. You see a few "horseless
carriages," but mostly, there are horses
and wagons. It's neat to see what
downtown was like so long ago!

Suddenly, it doesn't seem so neat.
There's a commotion in the street next
to you, at the First National Bank.
Before you know it, a man has grabbed
you and is pointing a gun at you!

"Nobody move!" the man yells.
"We're taking this kid hostage, and if
anybody tries to stop us — well, no
more kid!" You realize that these are
bank robbers — real desperados!

Turn to **page 48** *— fast!*

Terrified, you watch Buddy and some of his friends scurrying through the crowd.

Just as the men start running to their horses, Buddy and his pals flood the street — with marbles!

"Eeeeeoooow!" the man who was holding you cries as he tries to keep his balance. He lets go of you just before he hits the ground. You run to safety and watch as the police arrest the robbers. What a scene!

How can you thank Buddy for saving your life? You remember that you have your great-grandfather's watch. It's very precious, but so is your life. Buddy's grateful and tells you he'll keep it always and pass it on to his grandchildren.

Now, how can you get back to your own time? You go back to where you first met Buddy and just where the elevator *ought* to be, there is a large wooden supply closet. You open the door and step inside.

Turn to **page 49.**

49   The last thing you see as you close the door is Buddy, looking at the watch. Lights start blinking and then you're in an elevator! The door opens, and there's your mother, waiting for you!

You quickly realize that no time has passed in your world. Nobody knew you were gone. There's no way anyone would believe the true story, so you keep it a secret — the secret of 13. The only problem is explaining what happened to the watch. Your father is very annoyed that you "lost" it.

"That was a very special watch, you know. Your great-grandfather got that watch when he was a boy. Grandpa Bud — he was called Buddy by his friends — always claimed it was given to him by a boy he *said* disappeared into a closet one day after Grandpa Bud saved his life. It had something to do with marbles."

THE END

You're sure that what the man dropped was a cigarette! You're going to have to get back on that elevator and put the cigarette out. It may be the only chance of saving the whole building — if there *is* a chance.

You push the elevator button. The elevator you were on is now on 6, but the other elevator door opens. You step in. But where should you go?

If you think you can catch the other elevator on 6, turn to **page 54.**

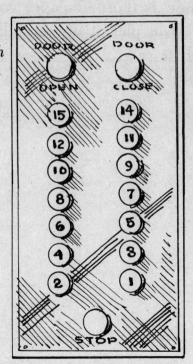

If you want to start at the top to find the other elevator, push 15 and turn to **page 57.**

If you want to hold this elevator on 1 until the other elevator returns, push the STOP *button and turn to* **page 51.**

51　　Good idea. You know for sure the other elevator will come to the lobby, too. And in the meantime, nobody can start a fire on this one.

It seems to take forever until the elevator with the cigarette and newspaper arrive. When the doors open, six people get off, grumbling and complaining about slow service. At last, you can get into the car. There, in the corner, is the newspaper you were holding. You pick it up carefully. Underneath it is . . .

Go on to the next page.

. . . a gum wrapper.

That man dropped a gum wrapper on the elevator floor, not a cigarette. You're no hero at all.

Carefully, you look at the newspaper again. It certainly does say everything you read.

Except for two things. The date *is* tomorrow — but it's not this year . . . it's the year before. And it's not the same town. Vaguely, you remember the weird tragedy when the Medical Arts Building in the county seat, 40 miles away, burned. Yes, that was just about a year ago, wasn't it?

So much for heroics. This is

THE END

Quickly, you push 6. By a miracle, **54** when you get there, the other car is still there. You rush into it and see that the fire is already smoldering dangerously. You know that the worst place to be in a fire is in an elevator, so you decide not to ride in it. Instead, you use the phone in the elevator to call the lobby and report the fire.

The doorman calls the Fire Department. While you are waiting, you spot a fire extinguisher near the elevator. Carefully, you look at the instructions and follow them exactly, pointing the spray at the base of the fire while staying a safe six feet away.

Within minutes, the Fire Department arrives. You, however, have already put out the fire. The firemen carefully examine the elevator. When they are convinced all the danger is past, they thank you and congratulate you.

Turn to **page 55.**

55   "You're a real hero," they say. "You don't know how dangerous an elevator fire can be!"

Little do they know.

The next day, the newspaper has a very different headline from the one you saw:

Proudly, you read every word of the article. It tells all about you, but it also gives some history about the building. It seems the Medical Arts Building was constructed 30 years ago on the site of the old Daily Bugle Building. The Daily Bugle Building had burned down. It was 13 stories high.

THE END

"I seem to be a bit confused," you
admit.

"Yes, you do. Well, sit down over here and tell me what happened right before you walked through that door." That seems like a good idea.

As you think about it, though, you realize that there's something wrong with your sense of time. It's not so much *where* you are, but *when* you are.

"What's the date?" you ask.

"July 1, 1912."

That's it, then. Somehow, you've traveled back through time! Is your mother going to believe this? Will you ever see her again to tell her?

If you want to try living in 1912 for a while, turn to **page 45.**
If you'd rather try getting back into your own time by going up the stairwell, go right through the stair door and up one flight by turning to **page 8.**

57   You want the elevator to go to 15 so you can start at the top and begin searching the floors one by one for the other elevator. The door closes and you begin the brisk ascent.

As the elevator passes 12, however, it suddenly begins to slow. You get a strange, dizzy feeling. What's happening?!

You feel as if you've been here before. You think you know what's going to happen — or do you?

Unexpectedly, the elevator stops — between 12 and 14. Could it be?

Yes, once again, you are on the 13th floor.

Turn to **page 2.**

"Hey, mister," you call politely.

"Yeah, kid?"

"I noticed you dropped something onto the elevator floor before the door closed. You know, you shouldn't throw garbage on the floor. It belongs — "

You stop talking because the man has walked out of the building. Then you remember the newspaper.

"Look at this, Mom," you say, reaching for it. But you don't have it anymore. It must have dropped out of your pocket in the elevator.

Yeah, in the elevator, where the man dropped something — probably a lighted cigarette! Suddenly, you know the story in the paper is true.

By now, you can smell smoke. Within seconds, firemen arrive. People wonder if they will save the building. You don't wonder; you *know* that, for the building at least, it's

THE END